When War Came To Town

AMY LAURENS

OTHER WORKS

Find other works by the author at
www.amylaurens.com

When War Came To Town

INKLET #32

AMY LAURENS

www.inkprintpress.com

Print ISBN: 978-1-925825-26-8
eBook ISBN: 9781393445982

www.inkprintpress.com

National Library of Australia Cataloguing-in-Publication Data
Laurens, Amy 1985 –
When War Came To Town
44 p.
ISBN: 978-1-925825-26-8
Inkprint Press, Canberra, Australia
1. Fiction—Fantasy—Historical 2. Fiction—Short Stories

First Print Edition: April 2020
Cover photo © Boykovi via Deposit Photos
Cover design © Inkprint Press
Interior art © Amy Laurens

WHEN WAR CAME TO TOWN

WHEN THE WOMAN WITH FLAME-coloured hair rode into town on the demon horse, nobody knew it would happen.

Sure, old Marley was ripped from his slumber in the room over the pub, dragged into the streets and flayed to within a half inch of death, but those kinds of things happened sometimes. All it took was a downturn in the economy, a few farms going sour, whispers in the wind of a witch, of black magic...

No. It was sad, ludicrous even, to think that people really thought Marley was clever enough for magic, but it wasn't the thing nobody knew could happen.

The bodies lining the street to see the woman, that was unexpected, the way they thrashed and elbowed and tromped, all trying to catch a brush of plate mail, or of the sharp, crackling hair of the deep-black horse. Unexpected, but also not that thing—not *It*. If people had stopped to think, they could have known she'd draw them to her like moths.

No. Not It.

The body, more meat now than human, with strips that hung from its limbs and a torso that still, days later, shuddered torturously in a parody of breathing as it lay caged over the square—that was a pity. Not a tragedy, because Virani had deserved, more or less, what he got—you don't steal from the Mayor's own treasury and deflower his teenage daughter without flirting with death as well. The flogging was perhaps a trifle unnecessary, as least to that degree. But still: not It.

Because the thing is, see, all these things are terrible. And if anyone had bothered to look into the eye of the demon horse as it pranced into town on Tuesday at dusk, they would have known immediately by the flicker of fire deep within that bad things were going to happen. And if they'd taken a moment to stare past the woman's captivating beauty with her hair of flames, they would have seen not the same flicker in her eye, but something worse. Much worse.

And so really, all the violence? While it surely wasn't expected, it also wasn't surprising.

So what, then, was It?

That one surprising thing that no-body knew would happen, that no-body could have predicted, that one thing that reminded everybody who they were and what really mattered?

That thing—it was Tikva.

Tikva, only seven, had joined the throng in the main street as the glorious woman on the coal-black horse had paraded past. She too had stretched out to brush finger against horsehair, and because of her small stature and resourcefulness in hiding behind an upturned crate, Tikva had succeeded where most others had not: she'd touched the demon horse.

Her fingers had crackled against the deep black fetlock as though electricity bridged the gap between them, and Tikva was left cradling fingers slightly burned with heat and a memory slightly singed with hatred, both of which meant it was she who'd first warned her mother that the horse was a devil, and because her mother was the town's wisest Elder, the rest of the town had listened.

It hadn't lessened their fascination with the woman, of course, or the horse. But at least afterwards Tikva could say she'd told them so.

But the strangest part of touching the horse hadn't been the realisation that it was a demon. The strangest part was realising that one day she too would ride into town on a horse like this, and all the world would come to see her pass.

She'd shaken her head, shoved aside memories and burned fingers, and gotten up. The crowds were closing now that the woman on the horse had passed. Tikva brushed the dirt from her undyed woollen tunic and pursed her lips. Mother needed to know about this.

That spark of connection when Tikva touched the demon horse was astounding, and by all rights and accounts it should never have happened—changing the course of history because it did—but still: not It.

Strange coincidences are sometimes possible, after all, enough so that while people note them, they are not utterly discombobulated by them. Some degree of chance, it is accepted, is part of life. Thus, not It.

When Tivka told her mother about the woman on the horse, Mother frowned as though she'd heard Tikva's father was back in town, and left the room abruptly to dig out her best shearing knife from the shed, oiling it with lavender and valerian before returning to sheathe it in the block in the kitchen, the kitchen wherein a steady troop of neighbours began and, in fact, continued until the moment Virani was condemned to be flogged in the square; wherein Tikva's night-time repose was plagued by feverish dreams in which she was torn from herself over and over and over again to be thrown into the heat of battle; and wherein she, Tivka, stood, a calm epi-centre in the midst of terror, and let the desire to fight wash over her.

It was some days since that first meeting when Tikva was sent down to the shop to buy more carrier oil for her mother, who had sold out of her famous calming tonic. Tikva eased her way down a street full of scowl-faced villagers, all ready to bite at each other at the least provocation, and climbed the steps to the shopfront with much relief.

Midway along, something nipped at her skirts. Tikva turned to see the demon horse tethered to the hitching post, being given an extra wide berth by patrons and street traffic alike. Tikva craned her neck to and fro, but there was no sign of the red-haired woman who'd brought trouble upon the town (so her mother said, and so Tikva felt it to be true).

Lip pinched consideringly between her teeth, Tikva stared at the great black stallion. The electric spark she'd felt last time—*had* it been a coincidence?

And if so, did it still matter?

And if not, then... what?

Breath held in her too-tight throat, Tivka reached for the horse.

His nostrils flared and his eyes rolled. Great, square teeth the colour of blood-stained bone nipped at her.

Tikva sniffed and rapped the stallion's nose. "No."

He stilled, snorting and shivering, ears flickering as he waited for her touch.

Tikva gave a satisfied nod and rubbed her thumb over the soft, delicate velvet of his nose. "Much better."

Footsteps sounded on the wooden steps and Tikva leapt away from the horse. She whirled and entered the shop before she could see who it was, hustling towards the oils with great concentration.

As Tikva neared the counter, Mister Avery lifted his green-striped apron from the vast expanse of his belly and wiped his face. "Well," he said gravely. "That is a concern."

"What's a concern?" Tikva asked in the tone of someone thirty years older and with as much expectation of being answered. Being her mother's daughter had its benefits.

"Virani was found with the youngest Miss Allum," Mistress Spector said, bosom heaving as she rearranged it on the counter. "And a rather large suitcase of the Mayor's own funds. The court has ruled for immediate flogging to be followed by imprisonment in the cage until death."

Tikva felt the blood drain from her face. This, this was the thing she'd been waiting for all week without ever knowing it; this was the culmination of all the whispered mutterings, the fights, the tiffs, the quarrels; this was the powder keg now lit, and someone had to stop it.

The bottles of oil clunked to the floor and rolled away under a shelf, unheeded.

But this was not It, because that thing we are waiting for, that It, was unexpected, and Tivka herself had known that something like Virani's flogging would be the natural outcome of the flame-haired woman's influence. And so, still, we wait.

As Tikva approached the square, she knew she was too late; the shouts of the whip master mingled with the agonised cries of Mister Virani, both a counterpoint to the bass harmony of the crowd's jeers.

Tikva jostled her way through until she could see the flogging post. For a brief instant, her stomach churned, but then she reminded herself that she'd seen worse out back of the butchers, and almost as bad on her mother's healing bench, where often she'd assisted. He shouldn't have tried to run away with Miss Allum—not this week, at any rate. Stupid, stupid man.

The whip master raised his hand to strike again at a thing already more flesh and bone than man. "No. Enough." Barely anyone in the crowd heard Tikva, and they never understood the authority of her words until much, much later, but at Tikva's command, the whip master froze. Beneath him, Virani shuddered and moaned, and for a moment there was a hush.

Then the crowd began to shout. "Why did you stop? Keep going! He's not had even two hundred yet, come on! Is your arm tired? I'll do it! Come on! Flog him some more!"

Tikva closed her eyes against tears that threatened to drown her fury, and reached out to the anger that filled the crowd.

Softly, she began to sing.

Peace, my child, now will rest
Upon your head while bluebirds sleep
Close your eyes and be you blessed
For peace abides here river-deep.

The words of the song unfurled through the crowd like blossoms, and slowly, one by one, people began to sing with Tikva.

It was only when the whole crowd lifted their voices together and Tivka could feel the harmony emanating from them that she released the whip master. He collapsed to the ground, shuddering, tears gushing from his guilt.

The demon horse pranced into the middle of the square, and the red-haired woman stared imperiously down from its back. "Who dares halt justice?"

Tikva tossed her head and marched forward, halting with folded arms in front of the horse she had no fear of. "I am the one you seek."

The woman on the horse started visibly as she stared down at the tiny creature in front of her, thin and small boned. She laughed, a sound that set the men in the crowd on their toes and the women on the arms of their men. "You are not the one."

Tikva tossed her head again for good measure. "Look me in the eye," she told the woman, "and tell me I am not."

Still laughing, the woman dismounted and strode forward, reins looped casually in one hand, hair rippling like flames in the breeze. She knelt down in front of Tikva, a smile dancing, and looked deep into Tikva's eyes.

Tivka knew the moment when the woman recognised her for what she was: the woman's eyes tightened, the fire dampened, and her whole body went stiff. "No," the woman whispered. "You cannot be she."

Tivka smiled, and it was the smile of swamp crocodiles when they corner unwary prey. "Oh yes," she whispered. "I am she."

And although she did not fully know what it meant, she knew without a doubt that it was true.

The woman stumbled in getting to her feet and stepped back a few paces before bowing curtly. "My Sister."

Tivka nodded in return, for even though her power was newly arrived, sparked into life by contact with the demon horse and matured by her act in halting the whip-bearer, it bore with it all the knowledge of the centuries; she could feel all the others before her who had worn the mantle of Peace, and she knew the truth of War's greeting: they were sisters now indeed. "Sister."

She send a trickle of her power outwards, probing at the edges of War's defence, and although they were locked as ever in a battle between two equals, she knew that right now, at this time, in this place, the battle was hers to win.

The other woman knew it too, and stepped back once again. "What do you wish done?" she asked, not deferential, but without the earlier command.

"You will go," said Tikva, a fact stated as simply as the colour of the sky, not a request, not an order. "And you will not return."

The woman nodded. "And him?" She gestured to the tattered lump of flesh that once might have been called Virani.

"He will hang in the cage, as the law decided," Tikva replied.

Around her, people muttered, and the woman called War raised her eyebrows. "From you, Sister? That is not what I would have expected."

"Peace too has a price," Tikva said in a voice that could sharpen diamonds, gaze never leaving the red flame eyes of War. "And this is my town."

War stared back thoughtfully for a long moment, then nodded. "I'll see you again one day," she said before swinging up onto her demon stallion.

"When you do," said Peace, "I will have a horse too. And I'll know how to fight."

War chuckled, a sound for their ears alone, and reached out to ruffle Peace's pale hair. "I'm sure you will," she said, not unkindly. "I look forward to it. Until next time, then," she added as she straightened in the saddle.

Peace nodded, jaw clenched tightly. "Until next time."

War's demon stallion reared his farewell, then galloped off into the gathering gloom.

Peace looked around the square at her town, and told them sternly: "Go home, and stop being ridiculous. I'll deal with you all in the morning."

The town, bowing to the wishes of a seven-year-old girl, recognising the authority of a millennia-old Power, did, and in the morning Tikva told them off, and that, of course, was It, because nobody could have predicted when War rode in that she would meet her match in a back-country town in the middle of nowhere, in the shape of a seven-year-old girl—and yet, she did. And that was It.

THE MAKING OF
WHEN WAR CAME TO TOWN

Some point, back in early 2010, I was really enthused about super heroes (like, more than usual, since I'm pretty fond of them at any given moment) and wanted to write some stories about them. It's probable that I'd been watching Will Smith's *Hancock* with my husband, actually. And somehow I conceived of this idea of having set of Powers, who were in perpetual chaos, fighting to keep the balance of the world.

Actually, I'm like 95% sure this was after watching *Hancock*, because if my memory serves me correctly there's a fight scene in the sky in that movie, and that was the fodder for a line not in *When War Came To Town*, but in *The Powers That Be*, Inklet #27, about the Powers battling in the clouds.

So. Superheros, known as Powers, fighting to keep the balance.

Forget, Inklet #39, actually came first, a lil flash-fic piece that I sold to Allegory Magazine in September of 2010. And given *Forget* is about Memory, one of the Powers, I decided it would be really cool to write, like, a cycle of short stories that all rallied together to tell an over-arching story about the Powers, but which also contradicted each other somewhat, and sometimes seemed to play on different timelines, or with—as it were—slightly different memories of how events actually happened.

The full cycle of stories never eventuated, though I still think it would be a cool commentary on the nature of memory and the way history is recorded, but this one, *When War Came*

To Town, would have been one of the first in the sequence, detailing a small event in the history of War, one of our main characters.

I like to think this event changed her a little; that she was just as shocked as everyone else to realise that the newest incarnation of Peace was just a child—and that, even though she was only a child, she still had what it took to stand up to a War who had decades, if not centuries more experience than her.

Maybe, this is the incident that humanises War again, allows her to remember that she too was once a human being—a realisation, or remembrance, that paves the way for the events of *The Powers That Be* a few decades into the future.

Read more by Amy Laurens!

DREAMING OF FORESTS

THERE WAS A FOREST. THAT WAS THE simple fact of the matter: there was a forest now, and there hadn't been before. Deena let the tent flap drop closed in front of her, inhaled steadily, and tried again.

Nope, still forest. She bit her lip, debating: go out and explore, or hide in the tent?

In the end, exploration won for the simple, practical reason that nature, as it were, was calling. So she caterpillared her way out of her downy sleeping bag, pulled her hiking shorts on over the black, fleecy leggings she'd slept in, zipped up her polar fleece jumper, crammed her grandmother's knitted beanie over her brown hair, and pushed her way outside.

The other tent was gone. For a moment, that made her pulse race—

but then the reality of her surroundings overtook her senses. The air inside the tent had been warm, musty. The air outside yesterday had smelled of the sea, a salty tang with just a hint of rotting seaweed.

Today, the air smelled like sap, and living things, a green smell she associated with her grandmother's garden thanks to that summer she'd spent there when she was twelve, when they'd spent hours of days of weeks pruning and twining and tending, returning to the house only for meals and sleep, hands crusty with black dirt her grandmother called gold, under-nails caked with the stuff, elbows and knees stained black—and green.

This, Deena thought, was what every green scratch-and-sniff thing should smell like. Forget your apple, forget your lime; *this* was green. She inhaled deeply, and despite the oddity of the situation, felt her eyes light up as her body relaxed, melting into the space while at the same time inflated, buoyed, full. Something about this wondrous, spontaneous forest was familiar—and right.

She had no idea what the trees were, but they were tall, straight as ship masts or indigenous spears, thick and thin, rough-barked but paler than stringy barks, a brownish-grey, and the tiny, emerald, coin-sized leaves looked soft as butter, soft as petals.

Deena had tried keeping plants in their third-floor apartment back home, but somehow she could never re-member to water them enough, or else she watered them too much and they died, thin and pustulant. She cried, every time, as her mother shook her head and made Deena walk them down to the communal skip bins in the alleyway behind the complex.

Her grandmother had consoled her on the phone each time, had promised that one day she'd have plants aplenty, more than she knew what to do with.

But one day wasn't soon enough for Deena—which was why she'd taken up hiking, of course. If she couldn't have plants at home, by golly was she going to surround herself with them in her spare time. So a forest? Amazing.

The other tent, her friends, vanishing? Less so.

Nature was still calling.

And the current cover situation was a little thin for her liking; yesterday, there'd been a handy thicket of salt bushes and something vaguely acacia-like between the grass and the sand dunes. Today, it was just open forest all the way down to the sand behind and to her right, and all the way up to the mountains ahead and to the left.

On the other hand, there didn't seem to be anyone else around.

Sighing, she attended to her body's needs, butt cheeks momentarily icing over as a wind whipped down from the mountain, setting the trees rushling and shushling—but it seemed like a freak gust and nothing more, and soon enough she was clothed and warm again—and hungry.

A brief forage in the tent revealed a couple of muesli bars tucked into the pocket of her raincoat, and of course, there were the packet soups in her hiking pack, and she still had a couple of litres of water. Nothing to heat it with, though; Rachel had had the Trangia in her pack, and some time in the night—as was pretty usual, these days—she'd snuck into the boys' tent, taking her pack with her for a pillow. Which meant that all of the above—Rachel, boys, tent, packs, and cooking stove—were now gone.

Deena sat heavily on the stump by the front of the tent and dropped her chin into her hands.

It wasn't that she'd never believed

in magic before—she'd seen her grandmother's garden, after all, and although she'd stopped protesting to the contrary so people would stop protesting her sanity, she knew full well she'd seen creatures in her grandmother's garden when she'd been little that had no right existing on this mortal plane.

But on the other hand, until now, magic had been content to merely linger in the background, a blurred, bokehed backdrop to real life, something vaguely sensed, but never fully realised.

What, Deena wondered, had made the difference today? Why now suddenly jump arrestingly into the foreground?

Or, she wondered, gazing around as the trees whispered secretively, why *here*?

Hmm. That seemed like a crucial question.

The tent, she felt, was light enough.

It would be a bit of a headache to get the whole thing into her pack with her camping mat—yesterday, Rachel had been carrying half the tent, but that clearly wasn't an option today, and neither was leaving the tent behind— but she should be able to manage. Because as she saw it, she could either sit here all day, hoping and wondering whether the others would come back—or she could go explore this magical, magical forest that even now was layering calm over her like blankets, like she belonged here, and *find out* what had happened to the others.

It took about thirty minutes, moving purposefully, to down a couple of muesli bars, swirl a packet of soup into one of the water bottles and gag it down, and pack up all the gear. It did fit in her pack—only just, and she'd had to let all the straps out, but it wasn't too heavy, just bulky.

And so, with the legs zipped onto

her hiking shorts, turning them into pants once more, with her heavy boots on and her beanie still crammed over her hair and her hands deep in the pockets of her emerald-green polar fleece jumper, and her dark blue pack sticking up over her head and weighing down her hips, Deena set off through the trees that had miraculously appeared, heading back approximately the way they'd come in the evening before.

Keep reading! Head to www.amylaurens.com/books/novellas/dreaming-of-forests/ to buy your copy now!

ABOUT THE AUTHOR

AMY LAURENS is an Australian author of fantasy fiction for all ages. She also used to be *lot* bossier than Tikva, and seems to have passed that trait on to her son. Oops.

Amy has written the award-winning portal-fantasy *Sanctuary* series about Edge, a 13-year-old girl forced to move to a small country town because of witness protection (the first book is *Where Shadows Rise*), the humorous fantasy *Kaditeos* series, following Evil Overlord Mercury as she attempts to acquire a castle, the young adult *Storm Foxes* series about love and magic and mental health, and a whole host of non-fiction.

INKLET #031
Welcome to Dark Dale
LIANA BROOKS

INKLET #032
When War Came to Town
A Powers Story
AMY LAURENS

INKLET #033
Not Fantasy
AMY LAURENS

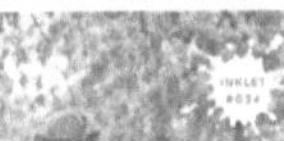

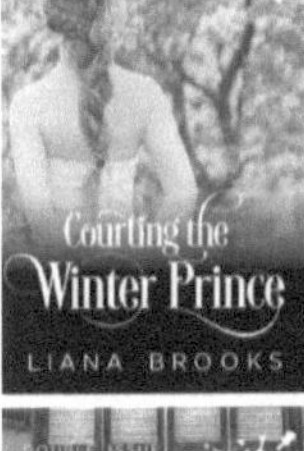
INKLET #034
Courting the Winter Prince
LIANA BROOKS

INKLET #035
At the Home of the Winter King
A Snow Foxes Story
AMY LAURENS

INKLET #036
With This Ring
AMY LAURENS

DOUBLE ISSUE
INKLET #037
Venus &
Seven Reasons I Said No
LIANA BROOKS

INKLET #038
OATH KEEPER
AMY LAURENS

INKLET #039
FORGET
A Powers Story
AMY LAURENS

INKLET #040
NOT QUITE Cinderella
LIANA BROOKS

INKLET #041
ONE BAD MAN
AMY LAURENS

DOUBLE ISSUE
INKLET #042
The Claustrophobia Of Loneliness &
Adam, Be A Star
AMY LAURENS

INKLET #043
The Artist as a Young Girl
LIANA BROOKS

INKLET #044
CONFESSIONS
AMY LAURENS

INKLET #045
But For Snow
A Kaditeos Story
AMY LAURENS

INKLET #046
The Boy Named NO
LIANA BROOKS

INKLET #047
Anamata
AMY LAURENS

INKLET #048
A Wolf FOR Christmas
AMY LAURENS